To

Ava,

Merry Christmas!

Love from

· ▶

to

Ava

Ava sees a present
wrapped up neatly with a bow.
The label says her name,
and the wrapping seems to glow.

"This present is for me!" cries Ava,
with the biggest grin.
She opens it to look inside,
and suddenly falls in!

Ava's in the frosty woods.
She can't believe her eyes.
To find a world inside a box
is such a big surprise!

ELF WORKSHOP

NORTH POLE EXPRESS

SANTA'S HOUSE

She stares up at a signpost
to see which way to go.
"Santa's house?" she says in awe,
then runs through sparkly snow.

Ava spots a village
and a family up ahead.
When she gets close she gasps because
they're made of gingerbread!

The daddy smiles at Ava.
"You want Santa's house, I guess?
You'll get there so much quicker
on the ol' North Pole Express."

NORTH POLE EXPRESS

SANTA'S HOUSE

Ava's at the station
when she spots a little elf.
The elf tells her, "I'm off to see
Santa Claus, himself."

Ava is excited.
"Yes, I'm off to see him too!
But I'm not sure which way to go.
Can I come along with you?"

They hear a distant chugging sound,
then see the train appear.
The elf says, "Ava, this is it!
The North Pole Express is here!"

ALL ABOARD, AVA

A small penguin conductor
brings the steam train to a stop.
"All aboard!" he shouts to Ava.
"Come ride with me up top."

NORTH POLE
EXPRESS

Ava has the perfect seat
and an even better view.
Snowy forests whiz by her,
while the chimney toots

"choo-choo!"

NOR

EX

They reach their destination.
Ava's face is full of cheer.
The penguin blows his whistle,
shouting, "Hooray! We are here!"

The elf takes Ava to a house.
Mrs. Claus greets her with glee.
"I'm so glad you are here at last.
Come in and sit with me!"

Ava sips hot chocolate,
and eats warm cookies from a plate.
The elf says, "Ava, we must go.
We really can't be late."

Ava is led through
a busy workshop full of elves,
where a million shiny toys
sit high on countless shelves.

"Will I see Santa?" Ava hopes.
"I think that would be neat."
The elf says, "Yes! That's why you're here.
He really wants to meet!"

"Ho ho hello, Ava!
You've been sooo good this year.
That's why I left a magic gift—
so I could bring you here!"

to *Ava*

"Yes, you wished to meet me.
I made that wish come true.
And now, I have a special toy.
One I made…just for you."

Ava peeks inside the box,
then quickly lifts her head.
She no longer sees Santa—
but is back at home instead!

Her trip has been amazing,
a night she won't forget.
And in the box is Santa's gift:
a North Pole Express train set!

Ava, hop onboard the
NORTH POLE EXPRESS!

Draw yourself and your friends
on the train to see Santa.

Written by J.D. Green
Designed by Jane Gollner

Copyright © Hometown World Ltd. 2019

Put Me In The Story is a
registered trademark of Sourcebooks, Inc.
All rights reserved.

Published by Put Me In The Story,
a publication of Sourcebooks, Inc.
P.O. Box 4410, Naperville, Illinois 60567-4410
(630) 536-1104
www.putmeinthestory.com

Date of Production: July 2019
Run Number: 5015149
Printed and bound in Italy (LG)
10 9 8 7 6 5 4 3 2 1

MIX
Paper from
responsible sources
FSC® C023419
FSC
www.fsc.org

put me
in the story®
Bestselling books starring your child!
www.putmeinthestory.com